The Pony-Crazed Princess

Princess Ellie
to the
Rescue

"Nice save," said Meg as Sundance walked forward again.

Ellie glowed with pride. Then she looked back at the woods. The face was gone. Maybe she had imagined it. But as they rode away, she had the strangest feeling she was being watched.

The Pony-Crazed Princess

Princess Ellie
to the
Rescue

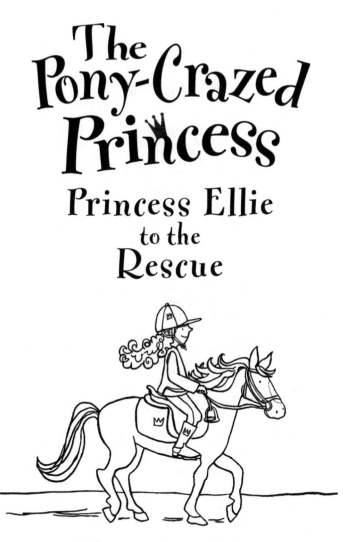

Diana Kimpton

Illustrated by Lizzie Finlay

USBORNE

For Jasmine

This edition first published in the UK in 2014 as *The Pony-Mad Princess: Princess Ellie to the Rescue* by Usborne Publishing Ltd., Usborne House, 83-85 Saffron Hill, London EC1N 8RT, England. www.usborne.com

First published in 2004 by Usborne Publishing Ltd.

Based on an original concept by Anne Finnis.
Text copyright © 2004 by Diana Kimpton and Anne Finnis.
Illustrations copyright © 2004 by Lizzie Finlay.

The right of Diana Kimpton and Anne Finnis to be identified as the authors of this work and the right of Lizzie Finlay to be identified as the illustrator of this work have been asserted by them in accordance with the Copyright, Designs and Patents Act, 1988.

The name Usborne and the devices ♀ ⊕ are
Trade Marks of Usborne Publishing Ltd.

This is a work of fiction. The characters, incidents, and dialogues are products of the author's imagination and are not to be construed as real. Any resemblance to actual events or persons, living or dead, is entirely coincidental.

A CIP catalogue record for this book is available from the British Library.
This edition published in America in 2014 AE.
PB ISBN 9780794534004   ALB ISBN 9781601303127
JFMAM JASOND/18 01423/14
Printed in China

Chapter 1

"Oh no," said the Princess as the book she'd been balancing on her head crashed to the floor.

Miss Stringle picked it up and sighed as she looked at the title. "Not again, Princess Aurelia. Perhaps you would find waving lessons easier if you practiced more instead of reading these silly pony stories."

"But I like them. And I like to be called Princess *Ellie*."

Miss Stringle sighed again. "I've told you before. That is not a suitable name for a princess." She held out the book. "Now, stand as tall as you can and try once more."

Ellie straightened her head, balanced the book carefully on top of it and set out across the room. The skirt of her frothy pink dress swirled around her legs as she walked.

"No, no!" shouted Miss Stringle. "Dainty steps. Not big strides."

Ellie slowed down.

"Now wave," said Miss Stringle.

Ellie raised her right hand slowly and waved at an imaginary crowd.

"And smile!"

Princess Ellie to the Rescue

Ellie pulled her lips back and showed her teeth. She didn't feel like smiling. She felt very foolish. No one in her pony books ever had to do anything like this. They had tons of friends, went to ordinary schools and spent all their spare time having fun with their ponies. All the things that Ellie wanted, but couldn't have. Sometimes Ellie hated being a princess.

She reached the other side of the room with relief and let the book slide off her head. "I'm finished," she said, as she caught it neatly. "Can I go now?"

Miss Stringle smiled. "Of course you can, Your Highness. Have a wonderful ride."

Ellie raced out of the palace classroom and up the spiral staircase to her bedroom. It was probably the pinkest room in the entire world. Her father, the King, had planned the decorations when she was born and he was convinced princesses liked pink.

Ellie didn't. She had managed to cover the pink walls with pony posters and bookcases full of pony books. But there was nothing she could do about the rose pink carpet, pink striped curtains and pink four-poster bed.

She threw off her dress and grabbed her pale pink jodhpurs from a closet. As she struggled into them, she glanced at the clock. She didn't want to be late. George was always grumpy when she was late.

Then she remembered. George wasn't there anymore. After caring for the royal horses for forty years, he had retired to a house on the beach. Today she would meet the new groom for the first time.

She pulled on her shiny black leather riding boots, thankful that no one in the kingdom made pink ones her size.

"It will be strange without George," she thought. "I wonder if the new groom will have as many rules." George had hundreds of them, most of which began, "Princesses don't…"

Ellie pushed her everyday crown on her head and picked up her riding hat. She paused  for a moment to straighten its gold and pink silk cover. Then she ran out of the room and down the back staircase to the stable yard.

To her surprise, there was no sign of the new groom. But there was a new horse. A beautiful gray thoroughbred looked out of the stall where George's horse had lived. She walked over to him and stroked his neck. His coat was as soft as velvet. The horse whickered gently and nuzzled her pockets in search of treats.

Princess Ellie to the Rescue

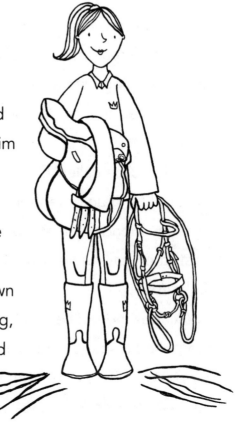

"Hello."

The cheerful voice made Ellie jump. She turned and saw a tall, slim woman walking toward her carrying a saddle and bridle. She had friendly brown eyes and her long, dark hair was tied back in a ponytail.

"I see you've met my Gipsy," said the woman as she put the saddle on the stall door. "I'm Meg. I'm the new groom. And you, I imagine, are Princess Aurelia."

Ellie nodded nervously.

"That's a real mouthful of a name," continued Meg with a smile. "Are you always called that or do your friends shorten it?"

"I like to be called Ellie," she replied, bravely. She didn't mention that she didn't have any friends or that everyone else insisted on calling her Aurelia or "Your Royal Highness."

"Alright then. Ellie it is." Meg grinned and pulled a sheet of royal notepaper from her pocket. "This note from your father says you want to ride Sundance today."

"Yes, please," said Ellie, hardly able to believe what she'd just heard. Meg was the first person to ever call her Ellie. Maybe everything would be different now. Maybe she could have as much fun with her ponies as the children did in her books.

"Then you'd better get him tacked up. I'll see to Gipsy and then we can be off."

Meg went into Gipsy's stall leaving Ellie open-mouthed with shock. George had never let her do anything in the stables. Although she had four ponies of her own, she had never been allowed to look after them. She knew tacking up meant putting on the saddle and bridle. But she had absolutely no idea how to do it.

Chapter 2

For a moment, Ellie wondered if she should ask for help. But this was the first chance she had ever had to do something in the stables by herself. If Meg realized how little she knew, she might not let her try again. "Tacking up can't be that difficult," she thought. "I'm sure I can figure out how to do it."

Princess Ellie to the Rescue

Ellie walked over to the tack room and hesitated. This had been George's special place. She could almost hear him saying, "Princesses don't go in there." But George wasn't around anymore and Meg had told her to get Sundance's saddle. It must be alright to go in.

Ellie stepped inside and breathed in the pleasant smell of leather. The saddles were on racks along one wall with the bridles hanging underneath. She stared at them nervously.

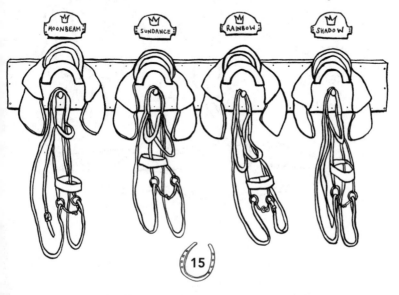

The Pony-Crazed Princess

They all looked the same. How could she tell which was Sundance's? Then she realized that above each one was a nameplate decorated with a golden crown.

Sundance's rack was so high that she had to stand on tiptoe to reach it. The saddle was heavier than she expected. The bridle wasn't, but it was hard to carry them both at the same time. The reins dragged on the ground as she walked across the stable yard.

Princess Ellie to the Rescue

"Hello, Sundance," she said as she went into the stall. The chestnut pony pricked his ears forward in a friendly way and walked toward her. His feet rustled the thick layer of straw on the floor.

"I'm tacking you up today," she told the pony. Her voice sounded more confident than she felt. She carefully put the saddle on the door just as Meg had done with Gipsy's. Then she looked at the bridle. She could recognize the reins and the metal bit that went in Sundance's mouth. But there seemed to be so many other straps and buckles. She wasn't sure which ones she had to undo.

"I'll just have to guess," she decided. She chose one of the buckles and unfastened it. The bit swung down and dangled by one strap. She had no idea if that was supposed to happen. So she picked another buckle and undid that one. The bit fell off completely and landed in the straw. She was sure that was wrong.

Sundance seemed to think so too. He put his head down and nuzzled the bit curiously.

Suddenly the door swung open and Meg came in. "How are things coming along?" she asked. Then she saw the pieces of the bridle and laughed.

Ellie felt so stupid that she nearly burst into tears. But she didn't want Meg to see her cry so she did the only other thing she could think of. She thrust the tangle of straps into Meg's hands, put on her most royal expression and stormed out of the stable saying, "Princesses don't tack up."

Chapter 3

As soon as Ellie was outside she felt even worse. She had always wanted to look after her ponies herself, like the children in her books. Now she had spoiled the only chance she ever had to do it.

She sniffed loudly and wiped away a tear with the back of her hand. Then she walked miserably along the stable yard to Rainbow's

stall. The gray Welsh pony was standing quietly with her head over the door. Ellie gave Rainbow a peppermint and stroked her neck.
The warm smell of horse made Ellie feel calmer.

She moved along to the next stall and saw Moonbeam, the palomino, quietly eating hay. Her mane and tail were snow white and the rest of her was a beautiful creamy gold. She came over when she saw Ellie and politely took a peppermint from her hand. Then she nuzzled Ellie's pockets looking for more.

21

Suddenly there was a loud noise from the end stall. Shadow, the black Shetland, had smelled the peppermints and was banging the wall to make sure he wasn't forgotten. Ellie ran over to see him. He was too small to put his head over the door so she had to reach down to give him his candy. She ruffled his mane and sighed as he crunched it. "I've ruined everything," she said.

Then she heard a clatter of hooves behind her. She turned around and saw Meg leading Sundance.

"I've tacked him up for you," she said, gently. "Do you still want to ride?"

"Yes, please," said Ellie, her voice unsteady from the nearness of her tears. "And I'm sorry I was rude."

"That's alright," said Meg. "It was wrong of me to laugh. I should have asked if you knew what to do." She pulled down the stirrups and held Sundance's reins. "Now jump on and we'll have a nice ride to cheer you up."

Ellie felt better once she was on Sundance's back. She leaned forward and patted the chestnut pony's neck while she watched Meg mount Gipsy. Then she followed her out of the stable yard and into the palace grounds.

As they rode side by side, Meg asked, "Did you mean what you said in the stable? You don't have to tack up if you don't want to."

"But I do," said Ellie, quickly. "I want to tack up and groom and muck out and

23

mix feeds and clean saddles and everything." Then she stopped and added quietly, "But I don't know how. George never let me."

Princess Ellie to the Rescue

"Then I'd better teach you," said Meg. "But first of all, let's have the horses gallop across this field. Unless princesses *don't* gallop."

Ellie laughed, happily. "This one does," she said.

"Follow me then," said Meg, and raced away on Gipsy.

Ellie squeezed her legs against Sundance's sides. The pony leaped forward willingly and galloped after the gray thoroughbred. Ellie leaned forward in the saddle and felt the wind whistle past her face. She could hear Sundance's hooves drumming on the ground as the pony carried her swiftly across the grass.

As they neared the other side of the field, Sundance started to tire. Ellie let him slow to a gentle canter until they reached the fence where Meg was waiting. Then they rode slowly along the edge of the field, letting Sundance and Gipsy get their breath back.

A fox trotted across their path. It stopped for a moment to look at them before continuing calmly on its way. Ellie watched as it squeezed under the fence and disappeared into a patch of woodland. She peered between the trees trying to catch another glimpse of it. But instead she saw a human face looking back at her.

Suddenly a bird flew out from the bushes and startled Sundance. He snorted with fear and jumped sideways. The movement took Ellie by surprise. Her left foot came out of its stirrup and for a moment she thought she was going to fall off. But she managed to stay in the saddle and soon calmed her pony down.

"Nice save," said Meg as Sundance walked forward again.

Ellie glowed with pride. Then she looked back at the woods. The face was gone. Maybe she had imagined it. But as they rode away, she had the strangest feeling that she was being watched.

27

Chapter 4

The pleasure of riding soon stopped Ellie from wondering anymore about the mysterious watcher. By the time they got back to the palace, she had almost forgotten the whole incident. "That's the best ride I've ever had," she told Meg. "I loved that gallop."

"So did I," said Meg. "Now put

Sundance in his stall and I'll show you how to take care of him."

First, Meg taught Ellie how to run the stirrups up to the top of the leathers and undo the girth so the saddle came off easily. Then, she showed her which strap to undo on the bridle and how to pull it off gently so the bit fell out of Sundance's mouth without banging his teeth. Finally, Meg handed Ellie a brush and told her to brush the saddle mark off the pony's back while she put the saddle and bridle away.

Ellie was blissfully happy. It was warm in the stall and it smelled of horses. For the first time, Sundance really felt like her own pony.

"Is there anything else I can do?" she asked when Meg came back.

"You can help me fill the haynets and water buckets if you like. But don't you have to get back for dinner?"

Ellie knew it was getting late but she was reluctant to leave when she was enjoying herself so much. "I have lots of time," she said, knowing it wasn't quite true. Surely it wouldn't matter if she was late just this once.

Meg took her to the barn and showed her how to fill the nets with armfuls of soft, sweet-smelling hay. "Make sure it's hay, not straw," she said. "It's easy to tell the difference. The straw has thicker stems."

The job took much longer than Ellie had expected and it was almost dark by the time they had finished. Meg went to hang the hay in the stalls while Ellie filled the water buckets. She had never carried buckets full of water before and was surprised how heavy they were. To make matters worse, the

water slopped around as
she walked so her
jodhpurs and
boots were
soon
soaked.

"You really need some rain boots," said
Meg, when she saw how wet Ellie was. "And
it might be a good idea to leave your crown
at home."

"It's just my everyday one," said Ellie. "Mom
and Dad would be upset if I didn't wear it. But
they might agree to rain boots. I'll ask them
this evening." Then she remembered. This
evening the Prime Minister was coming to

dinner. It was really important she got there on time. She'd be in real trouble if she was late. She glanced at her watch and panicked. "Oh no!" she cried. "I'm late. I've got to go." She dumped the last bucket in Sundance's stall and shut the door. Then she ran off across the stable yard.

"Thanks for your help," Meg shouted after her. "See you in the morning."

Ellie paused just long enough to wave goodbye before she raced over to the back door of the palace and hurtled up the stairs to her bedroom.

The clock beside her bed stared at her accusingly. Its bright pink hands showed she had only five minutes to get clean, changed, and down to the dining room.

The Pony-Crazed Princess

Ellie glanced at herself in the long mirror on the wall. She didn't look much like a princess at the moment. Her face was dirty, her hair was a mess, and her cheeks were red from excitement and exercise.

"There's no time for a shower," she thought as she pulled off her jacket and shirt. "I'll just have to do the best I can." She washed her hands quickly, wiped the dirty marks off her face with a wet washcloth and pulled the hay out of her curly, blonde hair with a comb. Then she popped her tiara on her head and slipped on one of her best dresses. It was a deep rose pink with sequins on the bodice and several layers of net petticoat under the knee-length skirt. Ellie's fingers struggled with the white satin sash as she tried to tie it in a bow behind her back.

As soon as she had succeeded, she ran down the spiral stairs and along the corridor to the dining room. Her feet were almost silent on the thick red carpet. She paused outside the door, smoothing the folds of her skirt as she tried to calm herself down. Then she stood up as straight as Miss Stringle had taught her, and went in.

The King and Queen were already at the table chatting with the Prime Minister. They all looked up when she arrived. But slowly their smiles changed to looks of surprise. They seemed to be staring at her feet.

Ellie looked down and groaned. Sticking out from the bottom of her dress was a pair

of very dirty jodhpurs and an even dirtier
pair of boots. She had been in such a rush
that she'd forgotten to take them off.

Chapter 5

Ellie wondered desperately what to do. Should she leave or should she stay? Then she made up her mind. She couldn't keep them waiting even longer while she got changed. She'd just have to act as if nothing was wrong.

Trying to look more confident than she felt, she strode across to the candle-lit table and sat down in her place. "I'm so sorry to have kept you waiting," she said.

To her relief, the Queen followed Ellie's lead. "Well, at least you're here now," she said, waving to the servants to bring the food.

Ellie was determined not to do anything else wrong. She tried hard to eat her meal in the way Miss Stringle had taught her. She chose the correct silver knife and fork from the gleaming selection by her plate, kept her mouth closed while she chewed, and only spilled a couple of drops of gravy on the crisp, white tablecloth. She even remembered not to drum her feet against the chair leg or play with her crystal glass while the adults talked politics.

At first the smell of wet jodhpurs and horse was hardly noticeable. But the room

38

was very warm and the warmth made the
smell grow stronger and stronger. By the
time they had finished their strawberries
and ice cream, Ellie was sure it was
impossible to ignore.

She looked nervously around the table to
see if any of the others had noticed. The
Prime Minister obviously had. When he
realized she was looking at him, he wrinkled
his nose and sniffed
dramatically.

"How are
things at the
stables?" he
asked with
a smile.

"Wonderful," said Ellie. "We have a new groom and she's going to let me look after my ponies myself."

"Really!" said the Queen with surprise. "And what exactly does that involve?"

"It's grooming and mucking out and cleaning tack and filling buckets and..."

"But that's work," said the King. "You're a princess, Aurelia, and princesses don't work."

Ellie stared at him in dismay. What if he wouldn't allow her to look after her ponies? What if he sent Meg away and got another groom like George?

"But it's much more fun than sitting in the palace by myself," she said.

"That doesn't make any difference," said the King, firmly.

The Prime Minister coughed gently to attract their attention. "Perhaps it makes it a hobby rather than work," he said and winked at Ellie.

Ellie grinned at him in delight. "That's right," she said, bravely. "It's definitely a hobby. And I'm sure princesses are allowed to have hobbies."

41

The Queen smiled. "I'm sure they are too," she said. "Provided they remember to get changed before they come to dinner."

Ellie was so delighted that she jumped up and kissed her. "I promise I will," she said. She decided not to mention the boots. It seemed more sensible to stop while she was ahead.

Chapter 6

The next morning, Ellie leaped out of bed as soon as she woke up. It was Saturday so there were no lessons. Instead, she could spend the whole day at the stable yard.

She was already dressed by the time the maid arrived with her breakfast on a silver tray.

Ellie ignored the perfectly boiled egg and gulped down the orange juice. Then she grabbed the buttered toast and ate it as she ran down to the stable yard.

"I thought you and Sundance might like a lesson today," said Meg. "But first we'll turn the others out into the field."

Ellie chose to lead Shadow. She thought he would be the easiest because he was the smallest. But she was wrong. Rainbow and Moonbeam walked quietly, but Shadow didn't want to. Every few steps he dropped his head to grab a mouthful of grass or dived into the hedge to eat tasty leaves. Soon, Ellie's arm ached from being yanked in one direction after another.

She was relieved when they reached the field. Meg turned Rainbow and Moonbeam

44

loose first. They trotted across the grass together, arching their necks and sniffing the morning air. Ellie watched them go. Then she carefully unbuckled Shadow's halter and took it off. But the little Shetland had much less energetic ideas. He didn't go anywhere. He just started eating the grass in front of him.

Back at the stable yard, Meg helped Ellie to groom Sundance. He seemed to enjoy it and lifted his feet willingly so Ellie could clean them out with a hoof pick.

The Pony-Crazed Princess

When his coat was gleaming and his hooves were freshly painted with oil, Meg showed Ellie how to put on his saddle and bridle. Then they set off to the riding arena for the lesson. It was a big area of sand with a wooden fence around the outside and some jumps in the middle.

Ellie had ridden in there many times with George but this time she felt very nervous. She was worried in case Meg didn't think her riding was good enough. She tried hard to keep her heels down and her back straight as she trotted Sundance around the arena. He wasn't nervous at all. He trotted confidently with his head up and his ears pricked forward. Soon, Ellie relaxed too and started to enjoy herself. Meg was a good teacher and quick to praise everything she did right.

"Now let's see how well you ride

without stirrups," said Meg.

Ellie was horrified. No one had ever asked her to do that before. "I can't," she said. "I'll fall off."

"No, you won't," said Meg. She helped Ellie cross her stirrups over the front of the saddle so they were out of the way. "Now off you go. It's not as hard as you think."

Ellie squeezed nervously with her legs and Sundance walked forward. Perhaps Meg was right. It felt strange riding without stirrups but it wasn't difficult.

"Now trot," called Meg.

Trotting was much harder. Ellie bumped and bounced so much in the saddle that she had to grab Sundance's mane to steady herself. As they went around the first corner, she slipped sideways and thought she was going to slide right off. Sundance stopped before she did.

"He's worried about you," said Meg. "He's stopping because he doesn't think you're safe."

"I don't think I am either," said Ellie, as she gave the chestnut pony a grateful pat.

"You're leaning forward. That's what's causing the problem. You'll find it much easier if you sit up straight."

Ellie felt more confident knowing Sundance was trying to help. As he started to trot again, she tried hard to keep her head up and her shoulders back.

It made a big difference. She didn't bounce nearly as much and she felt much safer.

Suddenly, she spotted a flash of green beside the barn. There was someone there. She turned her head to see better. But she accidentally leaned forward at the same time so she started to bump around again. She had to stop looking to get her balance back. She just had time to see a girl peering out from behind the barn – a girl who was watching her.

The Pony-Crazed Princess

Ellie was sure it was the same face she'd seen the day before. But she didn't have another chance to look until Sundance trotted back to that part of the riding arena again. By then, the watcher was gone.

Chapter 7

Ellie kept a lookout for the mystery stranger as she rode back to the stable yard. But she didn't see anyone. "I hope that girl's gone for good," she thought. "I don't like her watching me."

She untacked Sundance without any help and brushed away the mark left by the saddle. Then she led him out to the field and turned him loose with the others.

Sundance gave a playful buck as he trotted away. Then he rolled on the grass to give his back a good scratch. When he had finished, he stood up and shook himself from nose to tail before finally settling down to graze.

"Now it's time to muck out," said Meg. She gave Ellie a wheelbarrow, a fork, a shovel and a broom, and showed her how to take the manure and dirty straw out of Sundance's stall.

Princess Ellie to the Rescue

It was a completely new experience for Ellie. She had never tried doing such a dirty job before and, at first, the smell of the sodden straw made her wrinkle her nose. But she soon got used to it and worked her way slowly and carefully across the stall. When she had stacked all the clean bedding in a heap at the back, she swept the floor so everything looked neat and tidy. Then, feeling very pleased with herself, she set off to the muck heap with her wheelbarrow piled high with wet, dirty straw.

When she arrived, she realized she had to push it all the way to the top before she could empty it. There were some planks of wood to push the wheelbarrow along but it was still hard to make it go up such a steep slope. Her first attempt failed. The wheelbarrow just stopped halfway up and then rolled down again, pushing her with it.

"Maybe I need more speed," she thought. She pulled the wheelbarrow back far enough to get a running start. Then she raced at the heap as fast as she could.

The wheelbarrow shot up the planks, bouncing slightly as it went. Ellie kept pushing hard until suddenly the wheelbarrow dropped off the end of the last plank.

Princess Ellie to the Rescue

The wheel sank into the soft straw and the wheelbarrow stopped. Ellie couldn't. She bumped into the wheelbarrow which promptly tipped over sideways. She went with it, fell over the handle and landed flat on her face in the dirty straw.

Luckily, the muck heap was soft so only her pride was hurt. "Thank goodness no one saw me," she thought, as she struggled to her feet. But then she heard a sound. It was muffled, and stopped almost as soon as it had started, but she was sure it was a laugh.

Ellie looked around. Meg was still in the stable yard but the noise had come from the barn. There was someone in there and they were watching her. It must be that girl again! This time Ellie wasn't going to let her get away.

She ran toward the source of the sound, slipping and sliding as she came down the muck heap. As she raced through the barn door, she caught a brief glimpse of two legs disappearing through a window.

By the time she reached the window and looked out, there was no one to be seen. The watcher had disappeared again, but this time she'd left something behind. There was a piece of green cloth caught on a nail that stuck out of the wood.

Ellie pulled it off and looked at it. Whoever had been watching her had been wearing a green sweater. And now they were wearing a sweater with a hole.

Ellie wondered if she should tell anyone what she'd seen. But she decided not to. It was only a girl – a girl who had no right to be there. "This is my place and they're my ponies," thought Ellie. "I can handle this myself."

She pushed the scrap of material into the pocket of her jodhpurs and went back to help Meg.

57

Chapter 8

That night the weather changed. High winds brought dark clouds rolling in from the west and heavy rain lashed at the palace windows. In the morning, the noise of the storm made Ellie wake earlier than usual. She lay in bed wishing she could spend all day at the stable yard again. But she couldn't. She had to go with her parents to

Princess Ellie to the Rescue

visit Great Aunt Edwina who lived in a completely boring country house with no animals, no games and no TV.

Ellie knew she could ride when she got back, but that seemed such a long time away. She wanted to see her ponies before that. So she got out of bed, slipped into her riding clothes and crept downstairs.

She opened the side door quietly, pulled up the hood on her rain jacket and ran across to the stable yard. Gipsy put his head over his door when he heard Ellie's footsteps. He looked as if he had only just woken up. There were strands of straw caught in his mane from where he'd been lying down.

Ellie stroked the gray horse and looked across at the ponies' stalls. It was only then

she realized something was wrong.
Sundance's door was wide open.

She raced across the rain-soaked yard and
looked inside. But she was too late. The stall
was empty. Sundance had disappeared.

Princess Ellie to the Rescue

For a moment, Ellie was so shocked that she couldn't think what to do. Then she rushed back to the palace, calling for help.

Her shouts echoed through the building. Doors flew open in response and soon she was surrounded by maids, cleaners and secretaries, all asking what was wrong.

"Out of my way," shouted the King, as he pushed his way through the crowd. When he reached Ellie, he knelt down and hugged her. "What on earth's happened?" he asked, gently.

"It's Sundance," sobbed Ellie. "He's gone."

"Call security! Call out the guard!" shouted the Queen, who had just rushed up in her red velvet bathrobe and silk pajamas. Her everyday crown was perched precariously on top of her curlers.

Ellie led her parents down to the stable yard to show them the empty stall. The maids came with them carrying huge umbrellas to protect everyone from the pouring rain.

Meg was waiting for them. She looked as upset as Ellie felt. "I checked the stall just before I went to bed," she said. "He was definitely there then."

"He must have been stolen," said the Queen. "Whoever could have done such a dreadful thing?"

The King looked around carefully, as if he was searching for clues. "There's no sign that they went anywhere else. It looks as if they knew where Sundance would be." He paused and rubbed his chin thoughtfully. "That's strange," he said in a puzzled voice. "It must be someone who's been to the stable yard before."

His words sent a shiver down Ellie's spine as she remembered the mysterious stranger. "There's been a girl hanging around," she said. "I've seen her watching me and Sundance."

Everyone stared at her in horror.

"You silly child," shouted the King. "You should have told us."

Ellie burst into tears. "I wish I had," she sobbed. "I'm really sorry. I thought I could handle it. I never dreamed she'd do anything awful like this." She sniffed loudly and wiped away the tears with her hand in a most unprincesslike fashion.

The Queen swiftly passed her a lace-trimmed handkerchief. "Well, at least you've told us now," she said, calmly.

Suddenly there was a commotion on the other side of the yard. A soldier came in leading a girl by the arm. "I found her outside," he said. "She insists she wants to talk to the Princess."

The girl was about Ellie's age.

Princess Ellie to the Rescue

She was soaking wet and her long, straight hair was matted to her head. The zipper on her raincoat was undone. Underneath it she was wearing a green sweater – a sweater with a familiar-shaped hole.

"She's the thief!" yelled Ellie. She pulled the scrap of green material from her pocket and held it up to show it was a perfect match.

"I'm not!" shouted the girl as she pulled her arm free of the soldier's grasp. "I'm Kate. I'm staying with my grandparents. My gran's the palace cook."

Ellie stared at her suspiciously. "So why were you watching me?" she asked.

For the first time, Kate looked slightly guilty. "Gran told me not to bother you," she said. "But I love horses so much I just wanted to be near them."

The Pony-Crazed Princess

The Queen stepped forward and pointed at her accusingly. "Is that why you stole Princess Aurelia's pony?" she asked.

"I didn't take him," said Kate. "No one did. He got out by himself."

Princess Ellie to the Rescue

"Nonsense," said the King. "Horses can't open doors."

"Some of them can," said Meg, thoughtfully. She closed the stall door and tested the bolt. It slid backward and forward easily. "Maybe Sundance has just learned."

Kate rushed over and grabbed Ellie by the hands. "You've got to believe me," she pleaded. "I came to see the ponies really early before anyone was up. I saw Sundance undo the bolt with his tongue and run off, so I followed him. I thought I could catch him and bring him back. But he's fallen in a ditch and he can't get out."

Ellie felt her stomach knot with fear. She couldn't bear it if anything happened to Sundance. "What are we going to do?" she asked. "We've got to save him."

The Pony-Crazed Princess

"We'll send out a rescue team," said her father. He listened carefully while Kate described the exact position of the ditch. Then he shook his head. "It'll take a long time to get heavy lifting gear out there."

Ellie imagined how frightened Sundance must be. "We can't leave him by himself," she said. "I'll run on ahead and keep him calm."

"But princesses don't..." began her father, stepping in front of her to block her path.

"This one does," said Ellie, as she ducked past him and ran off into the driving rain.

Kate ran after her. "You'll get there quicker if I show you the way."

Princess Ellie to the Rescue

Behind them, Ellie could hear voices shouting "Come back" and "Be careful" but she didn't care. All that mattered was keeping Sundance safe.

Chapter 9

Ellie and Kate ran side by side up the lane and across the grass to the stream. Normally this was a gentle, babbling brook. But the rain had swollen it into a torrent. As their feet pounded across the wooden bridge, Ellie glanced over the side at the deep, fast-flowing water. She felt a shiver of fear. The rain would be filling the ditch as well.

Princess Ellie to the Rescue

"This way," said Kate when they reached the other side. She led them up a slope and then turned right into the woods.

To Ellie's relief, the trees gave them a little shelter from the wind and rain. She was already soaking wet and she was tired too. Running so far and so fast was hard work and she wasn't used to it. But she couldn't stop now. Sundance needed her.

They ran through the woods, twisting and turning between the trees until they came to a large area of sloping ground.

"Sundance is down there," said Kate.

It was difficult to run down the hill. Their feet slithered and slipped on the wet grass. But they didn't stop until they reached the ditch where Sundance was trapped. It was deeper than Ellie had expected. Its sides were steep and muddy. Large grooves showed where Sundance's hooves had slid in the slippery mud as he had tried unsuccessfully to climb out.

Ellie's eyes filled with tears when she saw the chestnut pony. He was completely exhausted by his efforts to escape, and was lying on his side in the shallow water at the bottom of the ditch. Luckily, his head was resting a little way up the bank, just clear of the surface, so he could still breathe.

"Sundance, Sundance," Ellie called. "We're here and there's help on the way."

72

Princess Ellie to the Rescue

The pony lifted his head slightly when he heard her voice, and whickered gently. Then his head fell back onto the bank and he lay still.

"He's too tired and weak to save himself," said Ellie. "He can't even stand up."

Kate nodded. "That's not the only problem. There's much more water in the ditch than when I left."

"And it's still raining," said Ellie with alarm. "If the level keeps going up, his head will be under the water and he'll drown."

"I hope the rescue party gets here soon," said Kate, nervously.

"So do I," said Ellie. "But we can't let him die. It's up to us to keep him safe until they arrive."

They slithered down the slippery bank

to where Sundance lay. Ellie gently stroked his nose and the pony flicked his ears slightly in response. "He's so cold and wet," she said. "We've got to do something to warm him up."

She took off her jacket and laid it over the part of his body that was still clear of the water. Kate put hers over him too and they both shivered as the rain soaked quickly through their sweaters.

Princess Ellie to the Rescue

"If we're colder, he must be warmer," said Kate.

Ellie had another idea. "I read in one of my pony books that a horse feels warmer if his ears are warm," she said. So they crouched down and rubbed his cold, wet ears, trying to warm them in their hands.

The rain continued to pour down and the water in the ditch rose higher and higher. Soon it lapped at Sundance's nose. The pony made a feeble effort to lift it clear. Then his head dropped back.

Ellie sat down in the mud and lifted his head onto her lap. Her legs were in the water now. It was freezing cold, but at least Sundance was safe for a little longer.

Kate sat down beside her. "Let's talk," she said as they huddled together for

75

warmth. "It'll take our minds off how cold and wet we are."

Ellie stroked Sundance's head and concentrated on Kate's voice as she described how her dad's job took him and her mom all over the world. She'd gone with them when she was small. Now she was older, she was staying with her gran and grandad so she didn't have to keep changing schools.

Princess Ellie to the Rescue

When Kate stopped, Ellie's mind immediately snapped back to the present. She realized with a shudder that the water had risen even higher. She didn't want to think what would happen if the others didn't get here soon. "Let's keep talking," she said. "It's my turn now."

She had just started describing a waving lesson when she heard a shout. She looked over her shoulder and saw Meg, her father and several other people waving at them. The rescue party had arrived. But were they in time to save Sundance?

Chapter 10

Meg slithered down the bank toward them. She was holding a wide canvas strap with a ring at each end. "We've got to put this around Sundance's tummy so we can pull him free."

Ellie held Sundance's head safely on her lap while Meg and Kate waded into the water, struggling to get the strap in position. It would have been impossible if he'd been lying on hard ground. But the mud which had trapped the pony was just soft enough to let them slowly wiggle the strap underneath him.

As soon as it was in place, the men on the bank let down a long rope with a hook on the end. Meg grabbed it and clipped it onto the rings. "We're ready," she shouted.

Ellie heard the roar of a tractor's engine and saw the rope pull tight. The strap around Sundance tightened too. The pony felt it and started to panic. Summoning the last of his energy, he started to thrash his legs wildly to escape the strap.

Ellie stroked his head. "Steady, boy," she said. "Stay still. It'll all be over soon."

Sundance flicked his ears toward her voice and grew calmer.

"Keep going," said Meg. "He likes the sound of your voice."

So Ellie kept talking. She told him how beautiful he was and how much she loved him. She talked about the warm stall waiting for him and the wonderful rides they would have together. And Sundance listened to her and lay still while the tractor pulled him slowly up the bank to safety.

As soon as he was out of the ditch, everyone rushed to help him. Meg started to rub him dry with handfuls of straw. The tractor driver put some blankets over him, and the vet listened to his heart with a stethoscope.

Ellie and Kate watched anxiously as they stood shivering in the rain. At last, the vet straightened up and smiled at them. "He's going to be fine," he said. "He just needs to get warm and have a good, long rest."

The two girls sighed with relief. Then Ellie grabbed some straw and went to help Meg. But the King took hold of her arm and stopped her.

"You've done enough already," he said. "You were naughty to run off like that, but you saved Sundance's life. Now you both need to get dry and warm yourselves."

"But I can't leave him now," said Ellie through chattering teeth.

"Your mother guessed that," he said with a laugh. "That's why she's put dry clothes and towels in the back of the Range Rover." He turned to Kate and added, "There's some for you too. And your grandmother insisted on packing hot chocolate and cream buns."

It was wonderful to climb into the car, away from the wind and rain. Ellie and Kate peeled off their wet clothes and wrapped themselves in thick fleecy towels. They rubbed their arms and legs hard to bring back some warmth into them and, as soon as they were dry, they pulled on their clean clothes.

Kate found the flask and poured out the

hot chocolate.
They sat together
warming their
hands on the
hot mugs while
they watched
the rescuers
helping
Sundance.
He was starting
to move now.
He lifted his head

to look around. Then, with a huge effort, he
heaved himself to his feet.

The girls joined in the cheers and watched
Meg lead him into the trailer behind the Range
Rover. Then they ate the buns to celebrate, as
she drove them back to the stable yard.

When they arrived, Meg lowered the ramp on the trailer, but she didn't go in. "You lead him out," she said to Ellie. "He's your pony."

Ellie ran into the trailer and untied Sundance. As she led him to the top of the ramp, she saw Kate looking at her. Ellie paused for a moment as memories of the last few days raced through her brain – the face in the woods, running through the rain, and huddling together in the ditch with Sundance. Then she made up her mind, took a deep breath and said, "I don't want you watching me anymore."

Kate looked embarrassed and stared at her feet. "I won't," she muttered. "I promise." She turned to go.

"Don't be silly," yelled Ellie. "I don't

want you watching me because I want you
to *ride* with me."

Kate turned back quickly. Her face lit up
with a huge smile. "Great," she said.

"Come and help then," said Ellie, with
a laugh.

Together, they led Sundance down the
ramp and into the waiting stall. Princess Ellie
felt blissfully happy. At last, she had a friend
to share her ponies with.

For more sparkly adventures of

The Pony-Crazed Princess

look for

Princess Ellie's Secret

Princess Ellie's Secret
Chapter 1

"Steady, Shadow," said Princess Ellie. The black Shetland pony she was riding pawed at the ground with a tiny front hoof. He was eager to start the dress-up race, and couldn't understand the delay.

"Are you all right down there?" asked Kate, with a grin. She was riding Sundance, Ellie's chestnut pony, who was much taller than Shadow.

Ellie grinned back. "Just you wait," she said. "Sometimes it's good to be small." She was so glad Kate had come to live with her grandparents, who worked at the palace. It was good to have a friend at last, and they had so much fun together with Ellie's four ponies.

"Are you two ready?" called Meg, the palace groom. When they both nodded, she shouted, "One, two, three, GO."

The two ponies leaped forward and galloped across the field toward two piles of clothes on the other side. Ellie leaned forward, urging Shadow on. But the Shetland's short legs were no match for Sundance.

Soon, the chestnut pony pulled ahead and reached Kate's pile of clothes first.

"Oh no," thought Ellie, as she saw Kate leap off and start putting on a long floppy coat. Then Shadow finally reached the other pile and she had to concentrate on her own part in the race.

Jumping off was easy – her feet were almost touching the ground anyway. Then she pulled on a long coat, wrapped a scarf around her neck and crammed a wide-brimmed hat on top of her pink and gold riding hat.

She glanced over to Kate, expecting to see her on her way back. But she wasn't. She was struggling to mount Sundance. Now that she was dressed up, she was finding it hard to lift her foot high enough to reach the saddle.

"We've still got a chance, Shadow," cried Ellie. She didn't have Kate's problem. Shadow was so small that she managed to jump into the saddle without using the stirrups at all.

She urged the Shetland into a gallop and headed back toward the finish line. Soon she could hear Sundance's hooves pounding after them, but this time the lead was too great. Shadow raced across the line just ahead of the chestnut pony.

"Ellie's the winner," shouted Meg.

"Well done," said Kate. "Being small was definitely useful that time."

Suddenly a voice called, "Princess Aurelia!"

Ellie looked around and saw Miss Stringle standing at the palace end of the field. She always insisted on using Ellie's full name. To Ellie's annoyance, so did almost everyone else in the royal household, especially the King and Queen. Ellie trotted Shadow across the field to say hello. But as soon as she was close enough to see her governess's face, she realized something was wrong.

"Whatever are you doing, Your Royal Highness?" asked Miss Stringle, giving Ellie one of her disapproving looks.

Ellie ignored the look and cheerfully replied, "We're playing mounted games. I just won. Did you see?"

"Indeed I did," declared Miss Stringle. "And I'm horrified to see you making such an exhibition of yourself. It is not suitable behavior for a princess."

Ellie felt confused. Surely there was nothing wrong with winning. Then she remembered the hat, coat and scarf. "I had to wear these," she explained, as she pulled off the hat. "You can't go in a dress-up race without dressing up."

"I am not talking about the clothes," said Miss Stringle, crossly. "It's the pony that's the problem. It's much too small." As she spoke, she waved her hand at Shadow. The greedy Shetland instantly assumed he was being offered food. He stuck out his nose and nuzzled Miss Stringle's outstretched palm. She pulled her hand away quickly and dabbed it clean with a lace-trimmed hankie.

Normally, Ellie would have been tempted to laugh. But this time, she was too full of indignation. "Shadow's not too small," she said. "He's exactly the right size for a Shetland."

"But that's not the right size for *you*," said Miss Stringle. "You look ridiculous. I'll have to tell your parents." Without waiting for Ellie to reply, she marched back to the palace with a determined look on her face.

Ellie's heart sank. Deep down inside, she

knew Miss Stringle was right. Shadow was her very first pony and she could hardly remember the time when he wasn't there for her to love. He'd been her best birthday present the year she was four and he'd been just the right size for her then. But over the years, she had grown and he hadn't. Now her feet almost touched the ground when she was riding him. She had hoped no one else would notice. What would happen to Shadow if she couldn't ride him any more?

To find out what happens next read

Princess Ellie's Secret

Also by the same author:

❀ Amy Wild, ❀
❀ Animal Talker ❀

Collect all of Amy's fun, fur-filled adventures!

The Secret Necklace
Amy is thrilled to discover she can talk to animals!
But making friends is harder than she thought...

The Musical Mouse
There's a singing mouse at school! Can Amy find it
a new home before the principal catches it?

The Mystery Cat
Amy has to track down the owners of a playful orange
cat who's lost his home...and his memory.

The Furry Detectives
Things have been going missing on the Island and Amy
suspects there's an animal thief at work...

The Great Sheep Race
Will Amy train the Island's sheep in time for her
school fair's big fundraiser – a Great Sheep Race?

The Star-Struck Parrot
Amy gets to be an extra in a movie shot on the Island...
but can she help Plato the parrot land a part too?

The Lost Treasure
An ancient ring is discovered on the Island, sparking
a hunt for buried treasure...and causing chaos.

The Vanishing Cat
When one of the animals in the clan goes missing,
Amy faces her biggest mystery yet...